For Joshua, Tabytha, Christopher, Jonathan, Cora Rose, Emily Claire, Thoburn, Nicholas, and especially for Jason, the very first Nimbus.

— S. B.

To my parents, Bob and Susan Oertel.

— W. S.

Published by **The Brookfield Reader**
137 Peyton Road, Sterling, Virginia 20165
Text Copyright © 2000 by Susan K. Baggette
Illustrations Copyright © 2000 Ward Saunders
1st Edition, 2000. All rights reserved.
Book design by Stephanie Glennan and schererMedia
Printed in Mexico

The Brookfield Reader

Baggette, Susan K.
    The night the moon slept / by Susan K. Baggette ;
illustrated by Ward Saunders — 1st ed.
    p. cm.
    LCCN: 99-78580
    ISBN: 0-9660172-8-5
    SUMMARY: A little cloud named Nimbus causes problems when he covers Mother Moon's eyes, causing her to fall asleep and fail to shine her moonbeams on the world, so Great Cumulus decides to give Nimbus a responsibility of his own.

    1. Moon—Juvenile fiction. 2. Clouds—Juvenile fiction. 3. Dew—Juvenile fiction. 4. Moonflower—Juvenile fiction. I.   Saunders, Ward.
II.   Title.

    PZ7.B14025Ni 2000   [E]
                  QBI99-1879

The Night the Moon Slept

BY SUSAN K. BAGGETTE · ILLUSTRATED BY WARD SAUNDERS

Published by The Brookfield Reader

Mother Moon stood on her pedestal of light across the river. She turned to her friend, wise Old Cypress, who sat cross-legged, dangling his feet in the river.

"I am so tired tonight," she sighed. "As I climb into the sky, may I rest for a moment on your branches?"

Old Cypress
nodded his mossy beard.
"Friend, lean on me."
So Mother Moon began her
climb, shaking her shimmering tresses of
silvery light. She glided to the uppermost
branch of Old Cypress and settled on her
friend's shoulders to rest.

Not far away, hovering high above the river, Nimbus, a mischievous little cloud, was out for a sailing lesson with his mother, Queen Cirra.

Nimbus was the youngest son of
Great Cumulus who lived with his family in
the Cave of Winds. Of all his cloud children,
Nimbus gave Great Cumulus the most concern.
Nimbus simply would not, could not behave.

His cloud brothers and sisters were all
helpful and useful. The younger ones
busied themselves blowing soft
summer breezes or made
shade umbrellas when
the sun's rays grew
too hot.

Others, in winter, scattered
millions of snowflakes over the
earth. The oldest and windiest
of all the cloud children
blew ships at sea to
safe harbors.

Little Nimbus tried to be helpful, too. But it was much more fun to play. Now as he followed his mother's billowy footsteps, he was unhappy and restless.

"Mind your manners and stay behind me," his mother said as they drifted high above the trees. "Maybe you will learn something new today." And off she swept.

But Nimbus was daydreaming as usual. Soon he dawdled far behind his mother. He saw two earthly boys below and hovered over them, watching as they raked a pile of leaves together. He thought how pretty leaves looked when they ran away from their trees and danced in the air.

So, just as the boys were about to dive into their sea of leaves, Nimbus mischievously blew the pile all helter-skelter!

Queen Cirra turned and warned him. "Nimbus, if you will not behave, I will send you home to the Cave of Winds!"

Nimbus tried to behave, but he still could not follow behind
his mother. There was so much to see and do.

Then he saw another earthly boy below him, running with a dog along a
forest path. Nimbus swept down for a closer look. He saw the boy was
wearing a tiger-striped cap with a tassel, and Nimbus wanted it. He blew a
sudden breeze behind the boy, making the tiger-striped cap fly high into the air.

Queen Cirra saw this and scolded him. "Go back to the Cave of Winds, little Mischief Maker, until you can mind your mother!"

So Nimbus turned and trudged back toward home, stopping to puff and kick at the air.

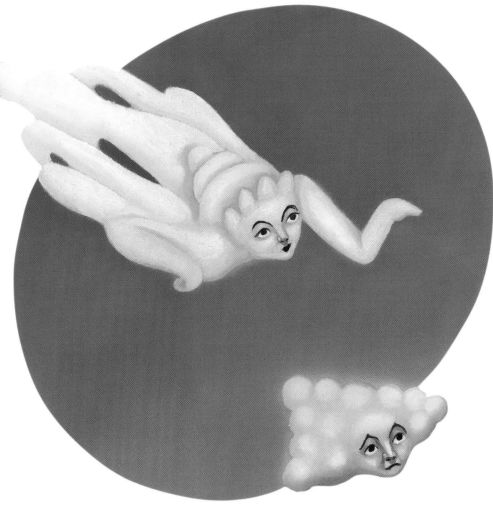

Then, from the other side of the river, Nimbus saw Mother Moon resting on Old Cypress. Her eyelids were drooping. She looked very sleepy.

Quietly he slipped through the night, skimming the sky as he crossed the river. He tiptoed behind her and surrounded her head with a dark, cloudy blindfold. Now, he thought, Mother Moon could take a nap.

Nimbus looked around the river. There were no little
boys hunting frogs on the riverbank because there was no
moonlight. The owls who always awakened at night and
looked for their dinner by the light of the moon were still
fast asleep. All the trees were nodding. Not a leaf
stirred. Even the river seemed to stop flowing.
One by one, the stars in the sky winked and
turned off their lights.

The night passed very slowly. Mother Moon was still fast asleep.

The entire forest was fast asleep, too. Nimbus grew restless.

The night air was chilly, and Nimbus shivered.

His nose tickled…

…and…then…he…sneezed!

He sneezed so hard that he blew himself off
Mother Moon. Now Nimbus was worried.
Were his forest friends unhappy because
they had slept all night? What had he
done? He raced behind some tall
oak trees and tried
to hide.

Mother Moon opened her sleepy eyes. She saw a tiny glow of light in the East beyond the river. Could it be her cousin, the Sun?

"What has happened?" cried Mother Moon. "Why, here I am, still sitting on the branches of Old Cypress. I didn't shine a single moonbeam all night!"

Wise Old Cypress looked around. Then he saw Nimbus

peeking out from behind the oak trees.

Old Cypress rattled his branches.

"I think Nimbus may have played a

trick on us and put us all to sleep.

Let's call Great Cumulus.

Something must be done about

his mischief-making boy."

Old Cypress leaned

toward Willow, his nearest

neighbor. "Call Great

Cumulus to the riverbank!"

All the trees whispered the

message until it reached the

Cave of Winds.

Great Cumulus heard the call. With all his majesty, he sailed to
the riverbank. Gathering his great white robes around him, he spoke.
"Who calls me from the Cave of Winds?"

"It is I," Old Cypress answered.
"You see before you Mother Moon, your lifelong
friend. Let her tell you why she is so unhappy."

"Speak, my dear old friend,"
Great Cumulus nodded.

"Great Cumulus," Mother Moon began,
"early last evening I was resting on the branches
of Old Cypress. Suddenly it got very dark, and I
must have fallen asleep. When I awoke, I saw my
cousin, the Sun, rising. I must have slept through the
entire night!"

A great, silvery tear slid down Mother Moon's cheek.

Old Cypress pointed a gnarled branch toward the tall oak trees.
"Perhaps Nimbus can tell us the rest of Mother Moon's story."

Great Cumulus blew a gust of wind up through the sky to summon
Nimbus. Slowly Nimbus appeared from his hiding place and shuffled
across the sky, trailing his little white robes behind him.
He settled quietly at his father's feet.

"My son," Great Cumulus asked, "do you know
what happened to Mother Moon last night?"

Nimbus whispered,
"Yes, Father. I saw Mother
Moon resting on Old Cypress.
She looked so sleepy. I thought if I
covered her eyes she could take a little
nap. But everything else in the forest fell
asleep, too. I'm sorry, Father." Nimbus looked
at Mother Moon. He felt terribly sad and began
to cry. He wept and wept.

Great Cumulus gathered Nimbus into his billowy arms and held him close. "My son, I can see that you are sorry for putting Mother Moon to sleep. I think it's time you had something important to do, just like your brothers and sisters. Before the sun rises each morning, you can sprinkle our forest friends with dewdrops to help them wake up and greet each new day. I'll even give you something special to help you remember when it's time to do your job."

Great Cumulus gathered a handful of his son's little tears and scattered them onto the riverbank.

Then a wonderful thing happened. Like magic, where his tears fell, up sprang tiny white flowers. They opened their eyes and blossomed, lifting up their trumpet-shaped faces toward Mother Moon.

"From this day forward," Great Cumulus spoke, "when night falls and Mother Moon begins her skyward climb, these little white flowers will raise their heads and trumpet to remind you that it's time to scatter your dewdrops. We shall call them Moonflowers in her honor."

And that is what we earthly people still call them
today. When the moon is shining, listen carefully.
You might hear their soft trumpet call.
"Nimbus! It's time to sprinkle your dewdrops.
It's time! It's time!"

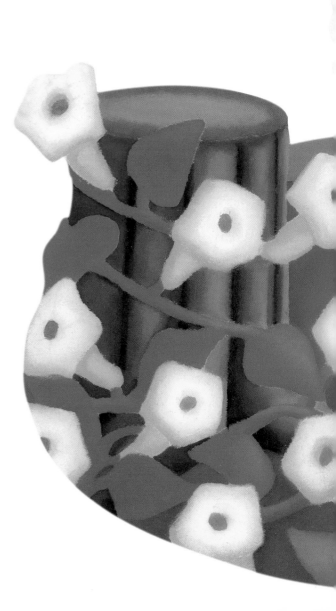

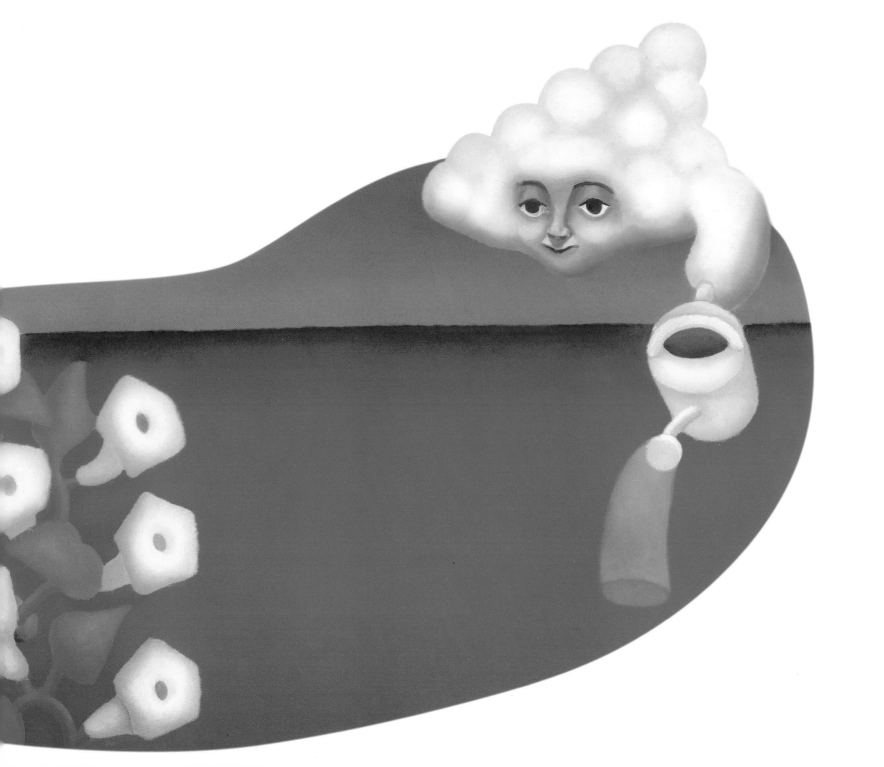